POKE OF THE TITANS

by MCM

1889
BOOKS

READ THESE OTHER ~~FINE~~ INSTALMENTS IN THE STEAMDUCK CHRONICLES SERIES:

1889

BOOKS

Published by 1889 Labs Ltd.
Visit our website for free books and other fun stuff:
http://books.1889.ca

For Yorick.
I knew him, Horatio!

AS IT HAPPENED, Andrew Carnegie's flying locomotive *did* run out of coal before they cleared Ohio; but luckily, Archimedes was able to save the occupants of his cabin by using the support staff as cushions.   Few that day would doubt his bravery, though to be fair, few that day would survive.

"Three hundred an' nine," counted off Finley the telekinetic fish as a short woman finished dropping 900 feet and became substantially shorter on impact, "Those life boats don't work at all, do they?"

"*Don't work?*" gasped Archimedes, "Wooden dinghies are not meant to work on anything but water, Finley!"

"Oh. Uh. Even if I told 'em to flap their arms?"

"I would think not," said Archimedes, "Still, no harm done.   Just another modest reduction in the world's criminal underclass.   Come, let's see if we can't find a gentlemen's club to retire to!"

Fig. 1: When making an emergency exit from an airborne locomotive, it is always recommended to have a telekinetic fish handy. Failing that, a last will and testament in a sturdy iron box.

Archimedes herded his fellow survivors and set off on a journey into the mid-afternoon sun. They soon found themselves in the vast spaces of the Western Ohio Desert, a place so remote and inhospitable that few survive long enough to draw it on maps.

Nearly two hours into their trek, Archimedes realized he should ascertain which of his companions would be the first to be eaten, as it would soon be dinner time, and there was not a restaurant in sight.

"Pardon me, my good fellows," he said to them with transparently-false joviality, "May I ask what professions you each employ?"

"I am a doctor of mechanical physics at the University of Boston," replied Dr Beschizza, wheezing badly due to his advanced age.

"I am a patent officer in Washington, D.C.," said Mr Johnson from the back of the group, his wooden leg slowing him down considerably.

"And I," beamed Captain Brownlee, "am a world-famous explorer and outdoorsman, able to extract valuable nutrients from rocks and dirt with my bare hands!"

"Excellent, excellent!" exclaimed Archimedes, and began contemplating which parts of Captain Brownlee would taste best with a mushroom sauce.

Fig. 2: Disciples of Mr Charles Darwin would object to the notion that a healthy human specimen could fall prey to a talking duck. On the other hand, they are largely monkey-loving deviants, so they may be dismissed out of hand.

Just then, they happened upon a small town, well-lit with oil lamps, and plucky music filling the air.   And there, standing before them, was a short man with a tall top hat and a face that suggested that smallpox had a big, angry brother with a vindictive streak.

"Good heavens!" Archimedes gasped, taking a step behind Finley, "I assure you, ruffian, we have nothing worth stealing!"

"Also, Brownie's got gonorrhoea," added Finley, "So no funny business."

"Oh my apol'gies, sirs," bowed the man, "I ain't be robbing folks for near on two months now.   I'm the Mayor of this here town!"

"And which town would that be?" asked Archimedes cautiously.

"Why Zuckerstown, of course!" beamed the Mayor, "Nicest little doo-dang you ever did saw."

Archimedes and Finley exchanged dubious looks, praying base-born stupidity was not as contagious as New Jersey made it appear.

Fig. 3: *The barriers to entry into the aristocracy are entirely relative to one's surroundings.*

"What is all that tubing for?" Archimedes asked, pointing to a long stretch of scaffolded ironworks, spreading through the town like a massive, tetanus-inflicting vine.

"That there's the Framework," replied the Mayor, "It c'nnects all them buildings together f'r... f'r... f'r stuff. An' stuff. Honest be, I dun not understand half the things Mr Zucker made round here!"

"Indeed," said Archimedes, "I should like to meet your Mr Zucker."

The Mayor became quiet and morose, and for a moment Archimedes thought the poor man had realized what he was.

"Mr Zucker died two nights ago," he whimpered, "cut right in two, like a chicken on Shearin' Day. Still don't know who done it."

"Ah. I see. Well, we should be on our way to another town..." Archimedes said, turning on his heel with a tip of his hat.

"Oh come on, duck!" teased Finley, "Don't be a baby! It's just a little murder! Live a little!"

Fig. 4: Scientists estimate that by 1900, all cities will have their sewers in above-ground tubing, in an effort to keep foul-smelling water out of reach of the poor, who mistake it for cologne.

Ignoring his instincts, Archimedes let his group be herded through town until they arrived at a grand old house with a sign out front that read: "The Titan Inn — Not a Brothel Since 1887".

"Bah. Shoulda slept in the desert," sighed Finley.

Inside, they were greeted by a buxom young woman with large spectacles and a face like an especially attractive constipated mule. She curtsied politely to her new guests.

"Welcome, gentlemen," she said, "I am Miss Klara, the mistress of the Titan Inn. If there is any service I can provide, do not hesitate to ask."

"—" began Finley.

"Silence, filthy fish!" snapped Miss Klara, her sweet smile never faltering. "Your rooms are all prepared for you. Are you familiar with the functions of the Framework?"

"Not at all," said Archimedes, noting the tubing all around the inn.

"Ah!" exclaimed Miss Klara, "It's quite simple, really. In each room are mechanisms that allow you to perform a great range of technological feats, such as person-to-person telegraphing, weather diagnosis, and photographic plate transmission!"

"Wowza!" said Finley, "Say, toots, I'd like a photographic plate of your—"

"One more word and it's fish sticks for dinner," Miss Klara warned.

Fig. 5: In special cases, a woman may own and operate a business, so long as she carries a six-shooter at her waist and demonstrates a predilection for mindless bloodshed.

Archimedes and Finley arrived at their room: a large space with a pair of luxurious beds, four brass oil lamps, and a suit of armour with its faceplate up, adorned with a little sign that read "Spittoon here, not the fruit bowl please".

"What d'ya think this is for?" Finley said, observing a massive piece of furniture that seemed to be built into the wall. Just as Archimedes leaned in to see, a small door in the panelling opened and an artificial hand popped out and poked him straight in the eye!

"Good heavens!" Archimedes exclaimed, pulling back, "I haven't been so abused since that gypsy woman stole back her jewellery!"

The appliance then spat out a small sheet of paper, with the writing: "You have been poked by Mr Johnson" in neat calligraphy.

Finley opened a small folding door to reveal a booth adorned with copper knobs, labelled variously with words like: "Poke", or "Write" and "Ignore". Then, to the side, a separate grouping contained the names of every guest at the Inn.

"Bugger me blind," cackled Finley, "It's a weapon of mass annoyance! I'm home, baby! I'm *home*!"

He began pounding on buttons like mad, and as Archimedes settled himself into bed that night, he was eased off to sleep by the sounds of countless cries of fright from around the inn.

*Fig.6: In some European countries, poking an acquaintance
in the eye is an acceptable form of greeting. These nations are
ripe for conquest, and should be shown no mercy.*

The next morning, there was quite a commotion around a nearby room, and Archimedes was forced to beat some commoners about the head with his walking stick to get a better view.

Inside, Dr Beschizza lay on the floor, his chest cut wide open, surrounded by a pool of blood shaped oddly like Finland.

"Oh dear!" exclaimed Archimedes, "He owed me five dollars!"

The Mayor arrived, handkerchief over his face, which Archimedes thought made him significantly more pleasant to look at. If only he could find a full-body handkerchief. And some perfume.

"This's terrible!" gasped the Mayor, "Just like Mr Zucker! Murdered innis room at night when nobody seen it, sometime after ten-thirty!"

"What happened at ten-thirty?"

"I fell 'sleep atta telescope."

"Hey duck," said Finley, wobbling through the crowd in a bleary-eyed stupor, "What's going — oh wow! Is that Finland?"

"Dr Beschizza was murdered, Finley."

"Oh is *that* what happened! And here I thought it was a game of charades gone too far. Say, let's pick his pockets. He owed me ten bucks."

Fig. 7: *There is a thriving cottage industry dedicated to the trade of blood spatter shaped like countries, the most valuable collector's card worth nearly two hundred dollars for a man whose remnants accurately depicted the Catholic nations of the world in a tidy row.*

"Do y'all know who mighta done this?" asked the Mayor.

"Well," said Finley, "in my experience, it's usually the Germans behind it. They run around saying *schnell* a lot, and to me that's about as suspicious as it gets."

"I see," said the Mayor seriously, working his single brain cell to its utmost, "Hey Harry! Go arrest Hans Mügenbrauer! He killed onna them guests!"

Archimedes grabbed the Mayor by the shoulders.

"Mr Mayor, I cannot express how dangerous it is to follow the advice of talking fish. They are notoriously untruthful, often only fit for political office or a role in a major news organization."

But the Mayor had made up his mind, and that afternoon Hans Mügenbrauer was hanged in the Zuckerstown square before a crowd of bloodthirsty townspeople, none of whom particularly minded the execution, because they, too, were unnerved by the word 'schnell'.

That evening, every patron of the inn received a healthy portion of bratwurst and schnitzel, pilfered from Mügenbrauer's home. But despite his best efforts, Finley could not convince Miss Klara to dress up as a German bar wench and dance on tables for him.

Archimedes went to bed that night uneasily certain of two things: that the real culprit had not yet been caught, and that Finley had followed through with his threat to defecate in the schnitzel.

Fig. 8: Like many ethnic dishes, bratwurst is often made from the remains of a loosely-defined set of meats, which the true gentleman knows never to enquire about.

The next morning, Archimedes went to submit a patent application for "a method of mutilating the vocal cords of fish using electrical currents and Jamaican rum" directly to Mr Johnson. But when he arrived at the room, he was shocked to discover the man who had previously been missing a leg was now missing a head as well.

"Wow," said Finley, "Removable limbs. Some people have the best ideas..."

Archimedes noted a letter opener embedded in the wall, and Mr Johnson's head embedded in the fruit bowl.

"Finley... are you thinking what I'm thinking?"

"Well yeah," said Finley, "But I don't think you can strictly call it a fruit salad if there are brains in it."

"No," sighed Archimedes, "I have a feeling Mr Johnson was murdered by the same villain that killed Dr Beschizza and Mr Zucker! Someone who obviously harbours a deep-set hatred of the upper class! A despicable transient sociopath!"

"Hey! *I'm* a despicable transient sociopath!"

"Yes, but more specifically, I hypothesize that our murderer is not, in fact, a fish at all, but a hobo!"

"Donkey Dung Jack diddit?" gasped the Mayor, who was suddenly at the door, "Harry! Donkey Dung Jack killed 'nother onna them guests!"

Fig. 9: *Honestly, some people will go to such great lengths to avoid civil conversation, it is really quite embarrassing.*

It took three tries before the angry townspeople could adequately hang the late Mr Jack, due to the noose slipping off his skin, coated as it was with several layers of the aforementioned donkey dung. Archimedes declined to watch the execution, as he found it difficult to engage in social events involving commoners.

That evening, Archimedes found Finley turning the pages of a massive book that was chained to the Framework Machine in their room. Just as he sat down for a glass of sherry, an artificial hand shot out of the wall and delivered to him an array of disc-shaped cards.

"Good heavens!" he gasped, "what are these for?"

"I'm building a game!" exclaimed Finley, "There's this instruction book that comes with the Framework that teaches you how. The game will be great… it's called Pokerous."

"How does it work?"

"It's basically just Poker, but you've got round cards."

"Bah!" spat Archimedes, "I refuse to partake in your copyright-infringing activities! Now stay quiet so I can take my repose!"

"Fine," grumbled Finley to himself, "I'll get Brownie to play with me. He always does a heckuva job."

Fig. 10: Leading scientists confirm that any product can be made more attractive if it is designed with rounded corners or a shiny white facade.

Fig. 11: While it is true that two minds are better than one, the inverse is more severe: if one of those minds is sub-standard, it damages the whole exponentially.

It should not have come as a surprise that, the next morning, Archimedes woke to discover Captain Brownlee had been murdered overnight. And yet, upon seeing the wily outdoorsman folded painfully in half in the middle of the street, Archimedes could barely contain his shock.

"So it wasn't a hobo after all," he sighed, "Anyone that has a problem with the upper class would obviously have no quarrel with Captain Brownlee."

"But he was a hero!" argued Finley, "He fought the Russian army to a truce with a two-by-four, and killed a pack of cougars with a bendy straw!"

"Yes, but not in good company."

"So we have no suspects?" asked the Mayor, arriving on the scene with all the grace of an epileptic sand crab on stilts.

"No suspects," Archimedes nodded, "No clues either. I'm afraid this case may go unsolved."

"That's just stupid!" growled Finley, "You're only saying that because he wasn't a fancy-pants douchemaster like you! It's not that there aren't any clues, you just don't want to look for 'em!"

"Nonsense!" spat Archimedes, "If there are leads to follow, we will follow them. Despite your insinuations, my fishy friend, we will give this case all the attention it deserves!"

And they did.

Fig. 12: It is a common fallacy that all good work requires one to move from place to place. Take, for instance, classical mythologists. Or prostitutes. Or classical prostitutes.

That evening, Archimedes was on his fourth glass of sherry when Finley revealed "Pokerous Version 2", which let you wager body parts as well as money.

"Given what has happened to our companions, I find your choice of features to be in poor taste! There's a murderer out there somewhere, and you're making an application that can chop someone's head off?"

"Don't get ahead of yerself, duck. Y'won't be able to pull a Johnson until version three at least. It's hard to aim the knives right."

Just then, Archimedes got to his feet, his eyes afire like the remnants of Donkey Dung Jack in the inn's hearth before dinner.

"Good heavens, Finley! The murderer isn't a person at all!"

"Oh, so we're back to accusing the fish again, are we?"

"No!" said Archimedes, grasping hold of the floating bowl, "No, Finley! It's not you, it's the *Framework*! Someone has built a killing application!"

"Nutters," grumbled Finley, "Late to the party again."

Just then, the Framework Machine rumbled loudly with the sounds of turning gears, and then, without warning, a massive artificial hand shot out from the doors, streaking cross the room, and smashing Finley's fish bowl into a thousand shards of glass!

Fig. 13: Young Dr Freud provided a caption for this illustration, but we decline to print it, as we are a respectable publication. Or… well… we know some respectable publications. Know OF them. Oh never mind.

"Mother of piss-gargling Jehosaphat," steamed Finley, barely able to hold all the water from his bowl in place with his telekinetic powers, "*Someone's* losin' a kidney for this, let me tell you."

A small paper floated to the floor, and written upon it were the simple words: "You have been SuperPoked by the Mayor".

Archimedes immediately stormed across town to the Mayor's residence, throwing open the doors and swinging his walking stick as if fighting hungry orphans.

"Ah, Mr Archimedes!" called the Mayor, getting up from his own Framework Machine, "Didja got my SuperPoke?"

"I did, sir! I most certainly did! And it nearly killed me, just as I suspect it killed Mr Zucker, Dr Beschizza, Mr Johnson and even that Captain fellow whose name I am trying to forget!"

"What?" gasped the Mayor, "Killed? But it's justa poke! It can't hurt a fly! The hand's only one foot tall!"

"Hardly!" mocked Archimedes, "The hand I saw was easily a full metre tall!"

"Oh no," gasped the Mayor, "Mr Zucker wuzza Europenean! He must've made the Framework in metric! I didn't know! What've I done? What've I done *dood*?"

Fig. 14: *Remember: it is only assault if the other party is brave enough to accuse you.*

"What you've done, sir, is cause me great indigestion," growled Archimedes, "I regret to inform you that I must remove myself from your town at once."

"But… but y'aren't angry 'bout yer friends?"

"Oh goodness, no.   Honestly, Mr Johnson was a cripple, and I long suspected Dr Beschizza had a mail-order doctorate, by the way he handled his dessert fork. And besides, a true gentleman never holds a grudge."

"Oh thank you, sir! Thank you!"

"However, there is one thing I would request, if you'd be so kind."

The Mayor fell to his knees, hands clasped together in a sad, begging posture; and for a moment Archimedes felt the overwhelming urge to call for the police to take him away. "Beggars never prosper" or somesuch.

"I want you to give me the ownership rights to the Framework and all its applications," Archimedes demanded.

And the Mayor did so, without delay.   He also removed the SuperPoke application from the Framework, until it could be revised and improved.

And so, as Archimedes and Finley set off from the Zuckerstown train station that evening, Miss Klara wept a single tear of joy — not simply because the damn fish was gone, but because she knew the bloodshed that had once threatened her town was finally at an end.

Fig 15. Often, women can be so overcome with emotion that, when saying good-bye for the last time, they will decline to look at you, or even acknowledge the fact that you exist. This is a sign of deep affection, I am told.

That is, until the Mayor sat down for a game of Pokerous Version 3.

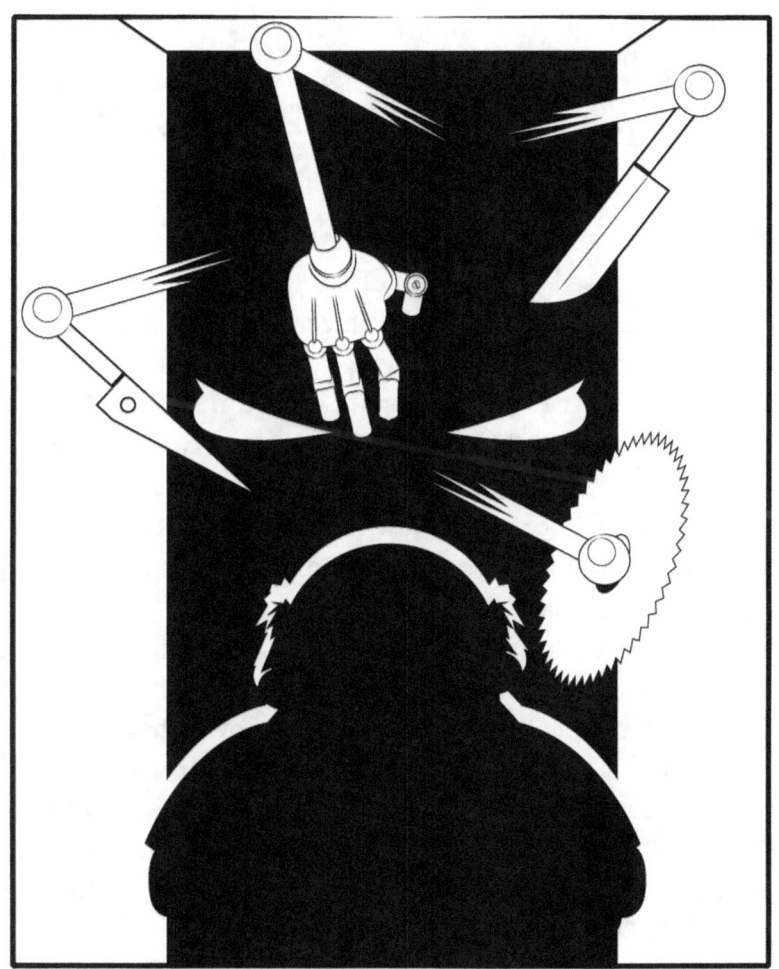

*Fig. 16: The rules are the same,
but the stakes are so much higher...*

Special Thanks

This book would not have been possible without the hard work and careful eye of the following ruffians:

Chris Gully, long-time conspirator and connoisseur of exasperated sighs.

Aidan, Mark and Snazzy, my Book Beta Test buddies who I believe wept openly when they read the PDF proof. (become a tester at http://books.1889.ca/beta)

Rob, Joel and John, who did not mind me ruthlessly butchering their 19-century selves for cheap laughs.

And, of course, **you**, the reader. Without you, none of this would be possible. You have no one to blame but yourself.

Also note:

You should also visit these sites because they are good and wholesome and excellent:

http://gadgets.boingboing.net — The best darn tech blog on the internet. Home of the Genius Non-sequitur.

http://xkcd.com — A must-read for any geek-minded individual. I parodied it here out of the greatest respect.

http://www.mashuptown.com — Mash-ups are an acquired taste. Acquire it, now!

WHO MADE THIS MESS?

MCM is the writer responsible for inflicting **The Pig and the Box** and **Panda Apples** upon humanity. When not writing books, he works hard on a cartoon show he created called **RollBots**. He lives with his family in Victoria, BC, Canada.